This book belongs to

Princess _____

The Royal Disney Princess Club

Every Disney Princess Treasures Her Friends

friendship

Story adaptation, crafts, and activities by Kris Hirschmann

Photography by White Light Incorporated, Bethel, CT

Design by Mark A. Neston Design

© 2008 Disney Enterprises, Inc. All rights reserved.

Published by Scholastic Inc., 90 Old Sherman Turnpike, Danbury, CT 06816.

For information regarding permission, write to: Disney Licensed Publishing, 114 Fifth Ave., New York, NY 10011.

ISBN-13: 978-0-545-03863-8   ISBN-10: 0-545-03863-4
U.K. ISBN-13: 978-0-545-08545-8   U.K. ISBN-10: 0-545-08545-4

Printed in Singapore

First printing, June 2008

Disney PRINCESS

Cinderella

A Storybook with Crafts & Activities

SCHOLASTIC INC.

New York   Toronto   London   Auckland   Sydney
Mexico City   New Delhi   Hong Kong   Buenos Aires

There once was a young girl named Cinderella. She lived with her father, stepmother, and stepsisters, Anastasia and Drizella.

Sadly, Cinderella's stepmother and stepsisters were not very kind. And when her father died, they began to treat Cinderella like a servant.

Many years passed, but despite the way she was treated, Cinderella grew into a beautiful, kind, and cheerful young lady. She made friends with the birds and the house mice, talking and singing with them to pass the time.

One day, a palace footman arrived with an
invitation. The King was throwing a ball that
night in honor of his son, the Prince. "By royal
command, every eligible maiden is to attend," the
Stepmother read aloud.

"Why, that means I can go, too!" Cinderella
exclaimed. The Stepmother halfheartedly agreed—
but only *if* Cinderella finished her chores in time.

At first, Cinderella was sure she could get everything done. But her stepmother and stepsisters gave Cinderella many extra tasks. They kept her so busy that she didn't have time to prepare her outfit for the ball. Cinderella was very disappointed.

What Cinderella didn't know was that her animal friends—Jaq, Gus, and the others—had spent the entire day turning a simple dress into a pretty ball gown for their friend. For the final touches, they added a sash and a necklace that Cinderella's stepsisters had tossed aside.

"Surprise! Surprise! Surprise!" they sang, as they presented the gown to Cinderella.

"Oh, thank you *so* much!" she cried. Then she put on the gown and ran downstairs.

The moment the stepsisters saw Cinderella's outfit, they grew absolutely furious!

"Why, you little thief!" shouted Anastasia. "Those are *my* beads!"

"And that's *my* sash!" shrieked Drizella.

The cruel girls began yanking and tugging on Cinderella's dress until the lovely gown was in tatters.

With nothing to wear to the ball, poor Cinderella had to stay behind.

Heartbroken, Cinderella ran to the garden and began to cry. As she wept, the air around her began to sparkle and glow; and right before her eyes, a kindly woman appeared.

"Dry those tears," said the woman. "You can't go to the ball looking like that." And then she held up a magic wand.

Cinderella's eyes grew large. "Then you must be—"

"Your Fairy Godmother," the woman finished. "Bibbidi-Bobbidi-Boo!" she said; and with a wave of her wand, a pumpkin turned into an elegant carriage. Cinderella's animal friends became stately horses, a coachman, and a footman. Finally, her dress was transformed into a beautiful ball gown, and her shoes became dainty glass slippers.

"Oh, it's a beautiful dress!" Cinderella exclaimed.

The Fairy Godmother urged Cinderella to hurry off to the ball. "But you must leave by midnight," she warned. "For after that, the spell will be broken."

At the palace, the ball was just beginning. The Prince stood dutifully greeting each of the maidens the King had invited.

Just then the Prince spotted a beautiful girl standing alone on the balcony. It was Cinderella. He rushed over to her and bowed, enchanted by the lovely stranger.

Cinderella and the Prince spent the rest of the evening together, walking in the palace garden, dancing, and gazing into each other's eyes. And before they knew it, they had fallen in love.

Cinderella was so swept away by the handsome prince that she lost track of the time. She was shocked to hear the clock striking midnight.

"Oh no! I must leave you," Cinderella gasped, pulling away from the Prince and running out of the palace. She flew down the grand staircase; but in her haste, she left behind one of her glass slippers.

Cinderella leapt into her enchanted carriage and drove away—just in time! At the final stroke of midnight, the Fairy Godmother's spell ended; and Cinderella, the carriage, and her animal friends were returned to their original forms.

The Prince found Cinderella's slipper; but not knowing her name, he had no way to find her.

So the next morning, the King ordered the Grand Duke to visit each house in the kingdom and to try the glass slipper on every maiden. The girl whose foot fit the tiny slipper would become the Prince's bride.

Upon hearing this news, the Stepmother locked Cinderella in her bedroom. Then the Stepmother slipped the key into her pocket and went downstairs to meet the Grand Duke.

Once again, Cinderella's mice friends came to her rescue.
They were able to steal the key from the Stepmother, push
and pull the key up the stairs to Cinderella's room, and finally
slip it under her door.

Meanwhile, downstairs, Anastasia and Drizella were attempting to squeeze their very large feet into the very tiny shoe. But it was no use. The dainty slipper didn't fit either girl.

Just then Cinderella appeared. "Wait!" she called, as she ran down the staircase.

The royal footman carried the slipper towards Cinderella. But before he reached her, the Stepmother tripped him. The glass slipper went flying and broke into a million pieces!

"Oh no!" the Grand Duke wailed. "This is terrible!"

"But you see," Cinderella said softly, "I have the other one." With that, she pulled the matching slipper from her apron and slid it onto her dainty foot. It fit perfectly.

The Grand Duke was delighted! At last, he had found the Prince's mystery maiden and true love.

But no one could be happier than Cinderella, whose dreams had all come true. The Grand Duke promptly escorted her to the Palace, where she and the Prince were reunited. They were soon married in a magnificent palace ceremony, and Cinderella and her prince lived happily ever after.

The End

Every Disney Princess Treasures Her Friends

friendship

This month's princess theme is friendship.

These crafts and activities will show you different ways
to treasure your friends.

Cinderella's Crafts & Activities

Cinderella would never have been able to attend the royal ball without help from her friends. Turn the page to discover Cinderella's crafts and activities all about friendship!

Royal Invitation

Make your friends feel like royalty with these Cinderella-inspired notes.

What You Need

- 8½- x 11-inch (22- x 28-cm) sheet of paper (any color) (**Hint:** Thick paper works well)
- Pencil
- Ruler
- Scissors
- Marker
- Crayons, paint, glitter, stickers, and other items to decorate your invitation
- Pink, purple, and gold paper
- White glue or glue stick

With a grown-up's help:

1. Set the sheet of paper on a flat surface. Mark the middle points of all four edges. Using the ruler as a guide, draw lines to connect the marks as shown.

2. Cut along the lines you drew to make a diamond shape.

3. Write a note to your friend in the middle of the diamond. Decorate the note with crayons, paint, glitter, stickers, or anything else you like.

Royal Idea

You can use stickers to seal your notes, if you like. Pretty stickers will make your friends feel like VIPs—Very Important Princesses!

Crafts & Activities

4. Fold in the four points of the diamond so that they meet in the center. You have now made an envelope.

5. Cut out a purple ribbon, a pink flower shape, and a gold crown, using the pictures below as guides. Stack and glue them together to make a royal seal.

6. Smear glue on the back of the seal. Stick the seal over the points of the envelope. Your royal note is now signed, sealed, and ready for delivery!

Friendship Ball

Use your special notes to invite your pals to a friendship ball! Dress up like princesses and dance the day away. Serve royal snacks, such as tiny sandwiches, tasty cookies, and tea. While you dine, chat about what you would do if you were real princesses. Use your imagination. Remember, anything is possible when friends work together!

Cinderella's Mouse Pals

Cinderella loves her friends—Jaq, Gus, and the other house mice and birds. Here's a simple, fun way to make your very own mouse pals.

What You Need

- Scissors
- Clean, no-longer-needed nylon stockings
- Eight extra-large cotton balls
- 6-inch (15-cm)-long piece of pink yarn
- Small rubber band
- White glue
- Two brown pom-poms
- Two wiggly eyes
- Bristles from a no-longer-needed paintbrush

To make one mouse, with a grown-up's help:

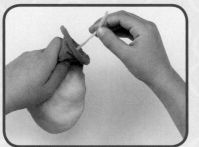

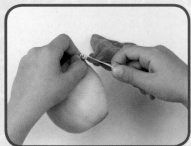

1. Cut the bottom 6 inches (15 cm) off one leg of the nylon stocking. Stuff the cotton balls into the toe of the stocking.

2. Tie a double knot in the end of the pink yarn. Poke the knot far down into the cotton balls.

3. Wrap the small rubber band around the stocking just above the knot in the yarn, tying the rubber band several times for a tight seal.

Crafts & Activities

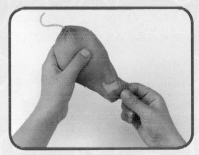

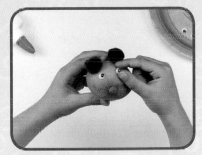

4. Turn the loose part of the stocking inside-out around the stuffed part. Pull it tight. You now have a stuffed ball with a pink tail on one side and some loose nylon on the other side.

5. Tie a very tight double knot in the loose nylon next to the stuffed ball. Cut off any loose leftover material. Your mouse now has a nose.

6. Glue pom-pom ears, wiggly eyes, and bristle whiskers onto your new friend.

♥ Royal Idea
Make lots of different mice out of tan, black, and white stockings or tights. Then share them with your friends!

Crafts & Activities

Nice Mice Friends

Your stocking mice want to be your very best friends!
These activities are sure to help you fall in love with
your new pals.

Name your mice.
Jaq, Gus, and Mary are three of Cinderella's mice friends. Use these names for your
friends, or make up your own.

Take your mice with you.
Your mice are small enough to fit in your pocket. Take them with you to the park, the
store, and other fun places.

Play with your mice.
Your little friends love to play! Include them in your games whenever you can.

Make beds for your mice.
Small cardboard boxes make perfect beds for your little
friends. Put cotton balls or some soft fabric in the bottom
so your mice will stay warm and cozy while they sleep.

Sing to your mice.
Cinderella's mice friends love to hear her sing. Your mice will love it, too!

Whisper secret wishes.
Your mice want to know your deepest wishes. Whisper your secrets
to your soft friends. Put them next to your bed at night so they can
share your dreams.

Crafts & Activities

What do *you* wish for? What about your friends? Pick your wishes from the list below, then ask your friends to do the same. Compare notes to see what wishes you have in common.

I wish for...

- ♡ Good friends
- ♡ A happy heart
- ♡ A grand palace
- ♡ Sweet dreams
- ♡ A lovely singing voice
- ♡ Inner beauty
- ♡ A magic wand
- ♡ An invitation to the ball
- ♡ Glass slippers
- ♡ A fairy godmother
- ♡ A beautiful ball gown
- ♡ My dreams to come true

Cinderella's Ball Gown

Cinderella needs a dress to wear to the royal ball. Make a beautiful gown for Cinderella, just as her little friends did in the story.

With a grown-up's help:

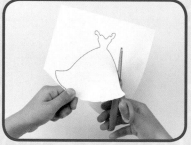

1. Lay the white paper on top of the outline of the ball gown on page 37. Trace the ball gown to make a copy. Cut out the copy.

2. Lay the copy on the piece of colored paper or card stock. Trace around the edges of the copy. Cut along the lines to make a ball gown.

3. Decorate the gown with glitter, buttons, bows, sequins, stickers, tulle, lace, or anything else you like. Lay the dress on the picture of Cinderella. Now she's ready to attend the royal ball!

Royal Idea
Use the copy to make as many gowns as you like. Make enough so Cinderella can wear a new dress every day!

Crafts & Activities

36

Be the Fairy Godmother

Play fairy godmother with your friends! Close your eyes and let your friends choose your outfit, shoes, hairstyle, and accessories. When they're done, admire your new look in the mirror. Then play fairy godmother for someone else. Soon you and your friends will look just like princesses!